BROKEN

The Vulnerability of a Black Man

SALEEM

Life Chronicles Publishing
Give your life a voice!

ISBN: 978-1-950649-51-8

Editor: Troy T. Landrum

Illustrations: Asiyah Davis

Cover Layout: Life Chronicles Publishing

Life Chronicles Publishing Copyright © 2021

lifechroniclespublishing.com

Table of Contents

Saleem

Dedication

I want to thank some significant people who have inspired, loved, and encouraged me throughout my life journey-

Dr. Charles Knox (you saved my life); RIP.

Duane Robinson (brother from another mother).

Rosa Barfield (the best laugh).

Sandra(Yahtzee)Bailey.

Edward, (Freshest).

Niela, (Roots).

Saleem

Most importantly, to all those who have hurt, scarred, and left me to heal on my own, I wouldn't know strength and courage without you.

STORY 1

What's Next

When I was twelve years old, I was caught in a house fire. I spent about four months in a burn unit, with third degree burns over ninety percent of my body. I also had severe lung damage from the smoke inhalation. As time went by, I got well enough to be released. Which should have been a happy time for me. Instead, it was one of sadness. Everywhere I went people would stare at me. Looking at the kid with all the burns. Pointing and whispering, awkward glances or even worst, giving me unwanted pep talks. I hated to go out, so I stayed in the house as much as I could. Though my mother knew it was unhealthy for me to isolate myself, she didn't want me to deal with all the questions and teasing.

We came up with an unspoken agreement. I would get fresh air as long as I wore my hoodie, gloves to cover my hands, and a ball cap to shield my face. It could be 100 degrees or we could be at the beach and that's how I would dress. I could be sticky and sweaty, but I didn't have to deal with the uncomfortable stares.

One day when I was sitting in the house, playing my tabletop Ms. Pacman game there was a knock at our door. I answered it and there stood a girl about my age, my height, and she had these pigtails in her hair. She was also skinny and had this gap in her upper front teeth. Before I could say anything, she said, "your aunt told me to tell you to come outside and wait with me on your front stoop until my mother comes and picks me up!"

She was the first person since the fire to just look me in the eyes, as though I was just a regular kid. I didn't know what else to say but, "ok." I begin to put on my gear. My hoodie, gloves, and hat. She said, "boy if you put all that on you will burn up out there!" I thought it was insensitive for someone to say that to someone in my physical condition. But before I could say anything, she said…

"If anyone bothers you, they will have to deal with me."

I looked in her eyes and believed what she said. I replied, "ok." From that moment on, we became friends.

Each day that we spent together she helped me to get out of my comfort zone.

I got so comfortable that one day we were running on the train tracks and hopped on a freight and rode it to God knows where. I wasn't afraid because I was with her and she wasn't afraid because she was with me. Our parents were so mad they had to drive to pick us up. When we weren't chasing trains, you could find us in the park, laying in the grass while looking up at the clouds playing the game, Can You See What I See?

"Can you see a mama bird feeding a baby bird? Can you see Winnie the Pooh eating out of his honey jar? Can you see Mount Olympus? Mount Olympus where? Over there."

On those clear days when there were no clouds in the sky, we would lay there in silence and our world would be perfect. The times she didn't come over to my house, I would go over to see her. I would walk through her door and whatever she was doing she would stop, run over to me and give me a big, hug. I would complain and tell her she is killing me. She would say to me, "shut up you know you like it."

One day while picking her up; she told me she had to tell me something very important. Something that she had been putting off for a while. She said, "D?" Which is her nickname for me. I have something to tell you... I am dying...I have sickle cell anemia with a trace of leukemia and the doctors say I may not live to see the age of fourteen."

"Dying??? You are not dying. You can't die! Dying is for old folks, dying is for relatives you hardly know, dying is for bad people who do bad things. You are not dying. You are going to live forever." I replied.

"I told you" she said, giving me a hug.

As time went on, I started to notice signs of her illness. There would be days she would be in so much pain that she couldn't get out of bed. She would lay in a ball and I would sit next to her, while she tried to rest.

We would watch her favorite movies over and over again.

For some crazy reason, she loved the Warriors. Every now and then she would look up to see if I had left. I would look down at her and make a funny face with a crazy sound. She would tell me to stop cause it hurt when she laughed.

For a while I tried to be her protector. I tried to shield her from anything that could harm her.

One day she snapped on me; she looked me right in my eyes and screamed, "I am dying! Do you understand I am dying? You can't stop that. Help me live now, have fun with me now or we shouldn't be friends!"

The last time I spent time with my friend, we sat on my Aunts second floor apartment balcony and we were watching the kids play with the water from the fire hydrant. Every now and then we would feel the cool mist when the breeze blew.

"D… that feels so good. You should be downstairs playing in the water not up here with me."

I didn't want to be anywhere she wasn't. Annet looked at me and said, "Do me a favor… go downstairs and play for me."

"For you?" I replied.

"Yes, for me, please." She said.

I raced downstairs and I stood under the balcony and screamed up to her. "ANNET… ANNET!!"

She screamed down "What!"

"What do you want me to do? Tell me what you want me do." I knew she was going to think of the weirdest thing in the world, but I didn't care.

"Walk in the water backwards and quack like a duck."

"Quack… quack… quack, "as I went under the cold water. When I came out, I screamed up to her, "what's next!"

"Do ten cartwheels in the water!!"

Each one I screamed "One… two… three…" when I was finished, I screamed up to her.

"What's next?"

She joyfully screamed. "Grab my little brother, take him in the middle of the water and hold him upside down. At this point her little brother only played safely on the outside of the gushing water. I looked at him, he tried to run away, and I yelled, "come here boy!"

I kept coming out of that water screaming, "what's next! What's next! What's next!"

I didn't care that people were looking at my scars. I didn't care if I was looking like a dumb ass, screaming up to my friend. I didn't care about the finger pointing and the whispering. I didn't care about anything, because my friend was happy. My friend was laughing. She was full joy. I swear to you I thought I was making my friend better.

I kept screaming, "what's next" until the Fire Department came and shut the water off.

One day I was walking from the candy store, eating a coconut flavored snow cone. I will never forget the feeling that came over me. It was like I lost something important, but I didn't know what it was, and that made me cry. In the middle of the sidewalk, I just started crying. I rushed to my Aunt's house and asked her to please call and check on my friend. My Aunt opened up her arms to me and said, "son your friend passed away a little while ago." I couldn't stop crying.

They wouldn't let me go to her funeral. They believed it would be too traumatic for me with everything I had been though. I truly never got to say goodbye to my friend.

There would be times I would be watching cartoons; I would just start crying. I would walk down the street and I would just start crying. I could hear kids laughing and I would start crying. I was always fucking crying. I went to my Aunt and told her that I can't stop crying.

I asked her, "what is wrong with me?"

She said, "son, you were in love."

I said laughing, "In love??? Love is for big kids. Love is for adults. Annet and I never even kissed. We hardly held hands. We weren't in love."

She said, "son, you experienced the most precious of loves."

I didn't understand then. I understand now, because I have been looking for my Annet. I have been looking for the one that could get me out of my comfort zone. I been looking for the one, that when we are alone and there is nothing to do, we are perfectly happy with each other's company. I been looking for the one that, when she doesn't see me in a while and I walk through the door, she stops whatever she is doing and rushes over and gives me a big hug. I will complain that she is hurting me, she would say, "shut up you know you like it." I been looking for the one who I am willingly and constantly asking, "What's next!? What's next!? What's next?"

Poem
Broken Heart Syndrome

When love ends prematurely.

Heart feels like an Anvil.

Once being fed, now starving.

Constantly questioning and reconfiguring.

Punishing the world, by being nonexistent.

Trying to rationalize the unfairness.

Questioning ones dopeness.

Trying to secure belief, there is a blessing in incompleteness.

Wishing your conscious would take a momentary absence,

for the caress of a stranger.

What is the wisdom of being alone surrounded by humans?

Or having a smile of a clown that fools no one?

Your eyes reveal secrets.

Peace

STORY 2

Coward

An old timer once told me, "If you want to hear beautiful things, ask someone to speak about themself. "Even if they tell you about their weaknesses, they will beautify them. Make them seem more like strengths than faults."

I am not going to do this with this story. I am going to tell you about the time I was a coward. About the time I let a good friend down. The time that I laid back and did absolutely nothing.

When I was incarcerated, that's a fancy word for being in jail. I was in cell number 747 and my good friend named Dave was in 746 right next to me. I knew Dave from the streets. In the hood, we were more of acquaintances. In jail, that made us best friends, because you didn't know who you could trust. The code was that you looked out for those from your hood.

Dave and I hung out all the time. We walked the yard together, played dominoes, and would work out together. Unlike myself Dave was no longer in a gang. He decided to give his life to God. He changed his way of thinking so he wouldn't end up back in prison.

Dave was a good brother, he tried to help the other inmates. He would help them study for the GED tests. If you were hungry, he tried to get you something to eat, to get you through the night. He was always talking to me about changing my life. Dave was a rarity in jail.

One day Dave and I decided to head out to the yard and do some laps, but we were running late. We get to the gate, and at that very moment the officer locked the gate. I could hear the click of the lock. I asked the officer in the nicest tone I could muster, "can we please get on the yard?"

He answered me with this dismissive and disrespectful tone, "fuck no, go lock back up, catch the next one!" Which pissed me off, to the point that I immediately lost my cool. I begin to call that officer, every version of cracker I could think of at that moment.

The vibe must have started to feel good to Dave. He started to chime in, and we started talking about the man's, mother, father, grandmother, grandfather, his children, dog, cat, and what he must be doing to sheep on his farm. The officer was hot, I mean beet red in the face. I swore I seen steam coming out of his ears. I wasn't worried because there was nothing he could really do to me. Dave and I left, laughing loudly as we headed back inside.

Once on the tier, Dave started to feel bad and decided he should head over to the chapel and ask God to forgive him for what he had just done. It wasn't the way a changed man should act, he said. I decided to take a nap and wait for the dinner bell.

Shortly after Dave and I separated, I heard something strange. Dave's cellmate was being told to pack up his stuff, he was being transferred immediately.

This was strange, because they usually give you a day or two notice in order for you to square away all debts and disputes, the administration didn't want no one getting killed because of miscommunication or money being owed. Since it wasn't Dave being moved, I really didn't pay it no mind. What got me up and curious was that they were moving someone right in. Which was something they only do in extreme cases, when they need to put an inmate in a safer environment.

In this case, they were moving someone in who was prison famous. I never met this guy in person, but I knew of him. One of the first people pointed out to me and warned to avoid him at all cost.

His name was Hacksaw, who was once the two-time heavy weight boxing champion of the whole state penitentiary system. Let me state that again... TWO TIME...BOXING...HEAVYWEIGHT...CHAMPION ...OF...THE...WHOLE...STATE...PENITENTIARY SYSTEM. He was even more famous for something else.

The moment I fully comprehended what was going on, I immediately went to my gang brothers. I told them that something must be done to stop this from happening. My brothers said to me, and I quote, "Dave is no longer one of us. His well-being is no concern of ours. If you do anything that gets any of us hurt, we will do the same to you. That's the code."

I anxiously waited for Dave to return. Knowing that all eyes were on me, wondering what I was going to do. I tried my best to throw Dave some verbal clues. Whispering to him, to refuse housing tonight. Which would cause him to go to segregation for a couple of months and upon his release we could bunk up together. Dave just looked at me and said, "I already know and I'll be fine."

After a few hours had passed and there was no commotion coming from next door. I figured that all was well, and the rumors were untrue. When they called for lights out, meaning turn all televisions and radios off to respect those who wanted to sleep. I relaxed in bed and begun to drift off. Then I started to hear raised voices coming through the vent. First it was just Dave's voice.

"Hey, Man, you don't have to stand that close to me, it's enough room in here for the both of us. Hey man back up a little, you don't need to be all over here. Hey man don't touch me like that, I'm not a woman player.

Hey man don't put your hands on me like that again!"

Then I started to hear Hacksaw's voice. This deep booming voice, that had this sound of excitement.

"O yeah you just like I like them. O yeah, I am going to enjoy you. Man, you are just like I like them."

Dave's voice:

"Hey man, I am a man don't be grabbing on me. Man, if you touch me again it is going down up in here. Man, you better kill me, because it ain't no way that bullshit going down! "

Hacksaw voice:

"Ooo.. You are going to give me what I want. You are, going to give me what I want. You are going to give me what I want."

Then there was this awkward silence, and deep down I knew that everyone in ear range was listening intensely, waiting for what was next. Then came the sound, that unmistakable sound of flesh hitting flesh at such a force. There was no doubt that something had been broken. I heard that sound over and over and over again. There was no doubt in my mind, that Dave was taking the beating of his life.

In between blows, Dave kept screaming out for help. Begging someone to call the guard and help him. I will never forget the pleading for someone to stop this man from raping him.

The louder he tried to scream, the more televisions and radios got turned up, louder and louder in attempts to not hear Dave's pleads.

At that moment, my cellmate jumped up. Mr. Righteous is what I called him. He was always talking about being better men. Protecting each other and becoming better humans.

I thought he was about to scream next door to Hacksaw, to leave that young brother alone. Instead, he just turned up my television louder to drown out the screams.

I wasn't so lucky, my head was right by the vent. I could hear every last word and sound. Every blow and rip of Dave's clothing. That sound, was the moment that I knew he was being victimized. I just laid there in disbelief. In silence, as tears ran down my face.

First thing that next morning, my gang brothers rushed to my cell, they had to inform me of some detrimental information for my safety. I quote them... "Dave is no longer considered to be a man. We are not to associate ourselves with those types, we no longer consider him to be a man. If we are found in the company of those we consider, no longer to be a man. The same fate may befall on you. That's the code."

As they were speaking, I could hear next door. All these so-called men, bidding on Dave and Dave's personal property. Stripping him of any dignity he may had left.

I wasn't sure who I was more upset at. Was it my brothers, was it these so-called men buying my friend's body and personal belongings? Was it myself for doing absolutely nothing? For being thankful it was him and not me?

I know what you are thinking, what could you have really done? You were locked up in your cell, plus your brothers warned you of any harmful interference. In all honesty, I should have at least tried. I could have started a fire inside of my garbage and set the fire alarm off. Then officers would have had to find where the smoke was coming from.

I could have taken a t-shirt and stuffed it into my toilet. Then kept flushing my toilet until water went everywhere. Then the officers would have had to investigate and figure out where all the damn water was coming from. I could have stood in my bars and screamed at the top of my lungs, "that I hate it here and I am tired of living in a cage. I am going to kill myself right now!" No matter what time of the day or night. The officers must come to check in on you. They have to get you a mental health counselor to avoid a suicide attempt. Any one of those three things could have brought an officer up to my cell. Maybe, just long enough for Dave to get the protection he needed.

I was worried about what may have happened to me for interfering, to be completely honest, I tried two of those three options before. Just to piss off the officers, and to see them run around. I knew any one of them could work.

I only caught a single glimpse of Dave after that night. He was standing inside of his cell. Dressed like a jail house woman with kool aid lipstick.

One day, a couple years later. I was free man, doing well in life. I wanted to see the old neighborhood, so I drove through. Sitting on his mother's front porch, was Dave. At first, I wanted to pretend like I didn't see him. We made eye contact, so I parked my car and headed over his way. We greeted each other with our phony smiles and seemingly warm handshakes. We played the roles of really caring about how each other was doing.

You know man it's good to see you, we need to hang out, go shoot some pool or something. I was acting mostly for Dave's wife and daughter. In his eyes, I could see him asking me, not to say anything about what happened to him in jail.

In my eyes I was asking him, not to say anything about not protecting him as best I could and that I broke the code.

The day of Dave's rape, I learned valuable lessons. First, a white man can use a black man as a weapon against another black person. Until that point in my life, it was hard for me to realize this truth. I would hear so many conspiracies about black people working with the system to destroy other black people. I couldn't really process that thought. I believed that black people were destroying ourselves, and there was no one else to blame. In my visual truth, I've only seen a black hand pass to another black hand a gun or drugs. I never once asked myself, who do you think supplies these weapons of destruction? It was clear to me now.

The second truth I learned that day. If you are not trying to stop the problem then you are part of the problem. Pretending the problem doesn't exist, or that it's none of your business, and using excuses like "it affects them and not me," "they shouldn't have been over there," "it is my family member and I don't want them to get into trouble," "what if they find out I spoke up?" These excuses allow the problems to continue, and to grow strength. One day it may bleed into your reality because it outgrew the very place it started.

The most important lesson I learned that day is that we must somehow find the strength, the resolve and courage to stand up against injustices and not be fearful of any repercussion.

If you can't find the strength or the courage to stand, then use your voice to speak out against injustices. Whether it be with a microphone or a piece of paper. If you cannot do that. At least, have it in your heart to pray or mediate on ways to remove the evilness from the lives of other humans. Just don't do nothing.

If you decide to do nothing. You can't ever get mad at the world. For not standing, speaking, or praying for you. In your time of need.

Peace.

Poem 3
No More Words

No more screaming Black Lives Matter.

Or writing about injustices.

When you cannot get off your ass and march in solidarity with your brothers and sisters.

No more speaking the names of our fallen heroes and heroines, pretending to shed a tear or walking in their footsteps, when every other word you speak is nigger or black bitches... promising to destroy the life of an African American...sssh...please not another word.

No more words of your false bravado. Pretending you are changing the world. Sitting at home, glued...! Watching your reality shows and are more emotionally invested in fictional characters survival.

Shedding Tears??

When Real Humans,

Brothers and Sisters are dying all around you.

You feel nothing.... nothing?

What is wrong with you?

No more changing your profile pic or ranting about the racist system. If you haven't taken one sincere, selfie less, powerful moment to stand hand in hand and shoulder to shoulder.

Like our ancestors did a thousand times before us and just walk.

One foot in front of the other.

Simple.

Let those who are truly trying.... SHINE.

Move so the real fighters can FIGHT.

Those who hearts are beating, LEAD.

Who spirits are lit, GUIDE.

Those who are not blinded by egotistical, brandnameism, I think I can capitalize off this tragic moment, buy my T-shirts I am selling in the corner. "look at me I'm walking with my people...say cheese."

No more!!!

No more pretending, play acting, false promises, inaction, posting events and not supporting, asking for finances on your endeavors but not helping another.

No more words.

Actions.

Saleem

Story 3
Broken

CHAPTER 1

Frustration

Sitting on the couch, his hand throbbing from pain, he could taste blood and strangely smell the mixture of fear and hate in the air. He often thought about this moment. He never believed it would become a reality. Just one of those "what if" thoughts, one of those thoughts that could possibly satisfy his memories of pain to make them go away. There he sat drenched in sweat and blood. Exhausted, confused, thirsty, angry, and sad. He glanced around the room trying to figure out exactly how all the damage was caused. He couldn't remember how he got inside. Flash backs in his head started to appear, knocking... no, pushing hard on the door. He was full of rage, a feeling that he hadn't felt in years. As he stood over the body, he could feel the confliction in his own body arise. The only person, he truly hated in this world. He could not piece together how the coffee table got broken, or how the flat screen television fell from the wall, or how the photos were lined up on the fireplace mantel. Nothing but twisted mangled garbage. Suddenly he began to have some idea of what was going on, which brought pride and shame to his heart.

He tried to warn his wife that something like this would happen, not necessarily the sight of someone beaten and laid out on the floor. More along the lines of, that nothing good could come out of them coming here. He left this place twenty years ago and promised never to come back. She wouldn't listen, she didn't understand the level of pain that lived in this house.

"I bet she understands now," he thought to himself.

He slowly moved through the carnage to find something to quench his thirst. As he passed by the barely breathing body, he could clearly see the bruises and handprints around the neck.

He was ashamed that he didn't feel bad. He felt a hand gently pulling at his ankle. He froze for a moment, rage welled up in him. He went from wanting a drink to an immense desire to kill.

His breathing became difficult and he could feel the sweat falling from his body, again. Somehow, he found the strength to just aggressively pull away.

"You will never hurt anyone again."

CHAPTER 2

Niama

The cab couldn't stop fast enough for her. She didn't know if she had paid her fare or not. A sickening feeling rose deep in the pit of her stomach. Thoughts of what her husband, the father of her children might have already done lingered in her mind. It scared her to the core. Her husband lived by absolute truths. He would do anything to protect his family. He was just as furious as he was gentle. He would give you the shirt off his back but would put hands on that ass for trying to disrespect or harm his family. The two qualities she loved and feared about him. As Nia made her way up the stairs, she noticed that the front door was partially opened. Her legs immediately grew weak, she had to use the handrail to pull herself up. The closer she got toward the opened door, tears begin to roll down her face. As she slowly stepped into the doorway, Nia was met by the sight of destruction. Just a few hours ago she sat in that very room, admiring the pristine condition it was kept in. Everything seemed to have its place, everything seemed to have its proper position. The photos on the mantle told a story of happiness her husband never spoke of. Now the room had nothing but broken glass, and furniture. Blood splatters on the walls and a body lying in the middle of the room. As she looked down at the body, Nia was filled with more disgust than care. She was filled with more anger than empathy. A part of her, wasn't surprised she'd walk into a murder scene.

By the look of it, death might have been the best option. Slowly she moved passed the semi-conscious body. The person lying there looked as though it wanted to say something. However, thought better of it once the person lying on the floor got a look at the anger of disgust on Nia's face. At that moment Nia didn't give a damn, she needed to find her husband. She found him standing at the kitchen sink, with a cup of water in his hand. He was looking out into the void, lost in his own thoughts. If it wasn't for the blood on his cloths and his bleeding hand you wouldn't have known that he was standing a few feet away from a body, nearly in a state of unconsciousness. She approached him slowly, they locked eyes and she opened her arms as she stepped closer and they embraced as if they haven't seen each other in years. Then they both started to cry. One cried out of regret and the other out of relief.

After that moment passed, she grabbed her husband's hand and led him to the guest bathroom. She sat him down on the toilet and began to clean his cut, all the while his head was on her chest and he was in total silence. There was nothing really to be said, both knew what happened in this house was awful. Both shared some blame. Both felt as though they failed each other.

CHAPTER 3

Revealing

Niama knew she couldn't lay full blame on him. He tried to warn her so many times. Damn near begged her not to make him come back here. He refused to give her a reason why they shouldn't have come, or why it wasn't safe for the family. She would have never imagined this is what he meant. She thought he was just worried about running into some over the hill enemies from the neighborhood, or just the random acts of violence that Chicago had become famous for, or even running into an old flame he had wronged. She, in a million years could not have imagined what happened in the house that day. The guilt began to well up inside her even stronger.

Why didn't she listen to him? Why didn't she listen to her husband? He has proven himself to be trustworthy. For twelve years, a damn near perfect marriage, and an awesome father. If he didn't want to come here, why did she push it?

She was lying to herself, wanting to believe that her children needed to know where their father grew up. In actuality she wanted to know why he was so afraid of the place he was raised. She wanted to know why every time she asked about his family, he would change the subject. This was the only part of himself he had kept hidden from her. She needed to know what was causing the nightmares that woke him up with tears in his eyes. In a way, she wanted to help him fix the one part of him she couldn't reach. Even though he constantly told her that he was fine, she could feel his pain.

She carefully led him to their crowded bedroom, even though his sister told them they could have the entire downstairs to themselves, which had an extra bedroom for their boys. He insisted on them all sleeping in the same room together. She carefully pulled off his blood-stained clothes, got him some fresh ones out of their suitcase, and put the bloody ones in a plastic bag. They could hear the struggling of the body on the floor, as though someone was trying to get up. They laid down and both of them looked out of window. They stared at the dusk sky. Raheem begun to speak for the first time since she arrived.

CHAPTER 4

Just a Baby

There was a full moon the first night. I was lying in bed calling myself playing peek a boo with the moon. I had to be no more than four or five. Thinking about it now makes me laugh. I kept putting my pillow over my face and peeking out to see if the moon was still watching me. I screamed at the moon "peek a boo!" It was like I knew that moment was the last time I would truly be a child. I was holding onto that last moment as long as I could. Once my bedroom door cracked open, I knew something was wrong. I watched as this figure slowly moved across my room. At first, I thought it was going to yell at me for being up past my bedtime and it was going to give me that, "You know what give me that, I will beat your ass if you don't go to sleep, speech." Instead, it grabbed my hand, pulled me out of bed and placed a finger on my mouth signaling me to be quiet. I was a little scared and excited at the same time.

I thought I was either going to get a surprise late night snack or get my ass beat.

Either way, I knew that I was going to see what the mysterious night life held. I was led by the hand into a big bedroom. Which seemed to be different at night for some reason. I mean everything looked so different to me, even the little black and white television that I watched daytime cartoons on. I could remember looking at Jackie Gleason where Casper the Ghost was supposed to be. I heard the crowd laughing at a joke that I missed. I watched this big white man move around this room screaming in pain from his hand getting hit. I couldn't help but to laugh.

It took me a moment to notice the knife to my throat. The words that followed have never left me. "You will do as I say, or I will cut your throat, place you in a trash bag and throw you away. No one will ever find you!" I don't think I have ever felt so much fear. The crazy part is, it wasn't the knife that I feared. It was the intense look that told me, I was in trouble. I knew if I didn't listen the worst would happen to me. I watched as she disrobed herself and stood in front of me. I can still smell her to this day. I can still hear her words as she told me what to do. I can still feel the shame that filled me. When I thought it was over, it actually was the beginning.

She grabbed an extension cord that was connected to the television and began to beat me. Calling me all sorts of nasty , disgusting, and sick names. She told me if I tell anyone, no one will believe me, and she will do worst. Beat me more and then kill me. She made me drink down Listerine, it burned my throat. Only after that was, I allowed to go to bed, I ran as fast as I could and hid myself from the moon.

The next morning, I was, covered in welts and bruises from her beating. My body sore and I was terrified to come out of my room, in fear of what was waiting for me on the other side of the door.

I was called into kitchen by her to eat breakfast. Was it a coincidence that she fixed my favorite, pancakes? That is why to this day I can't stomach them. That morning, I didn't have an appetite, I couldn't eat sitting across from her. She sat there smiling at me... Like fucking pancakes was going to make me forgive and forget what was done. I had no more joy inside of me, I didn't realize it then, my innocence had been stolen. From that moment on I could no longer trust my mother.

CHAPTER 5

Understanding

He could feel Nia's hands tightening around him, as she laid quietly in his arms. He could feel her tear drops falling onto his skin. It was hurting him to know that his words were hurting her. Raheem realized he should have told her the stories a long time ago. He was afraid to lose her. Not as his wife, he knew without a doubt that she loved him, but as his friend, his fun partner. He was afraid that if she found out about his past, with all the abuse and pain he had suffered that it would change things between them. That it would be some sort of red flag that would make her keep her distance. It would change the way she looked at him, her looks that filled him with passion, this attraction and sense of confidence that he never received from anyone else. He loved the way she called his name. Her voice was always filled with love and assurance. Making him feel loved and wanted.

He never wanted Niama to look at him or call on him any differently. He never wanted her to look at him with pity that people placed on those who dealt with homelessness, or the way someone looks at animals in an animal shelter. All the while contemplating whether or not to give them a home. That phony sadness and remorse. He didn't want Niama to see him as someone she should feel sorry for or worry that his past would one day hurt her.

When they met, for the first time in his life he began to have real hope. He began to gain strength and it revealed to him that he was ready to love, to trust and be trustworthy. He could see a future with peace and happiness. Raheem survived the life of noise and sadness, he didn't want to risk losing the chance to love. He thought that it would be for the best, to keep his childhood a secret. Raheem gave her complete access to everything else about him. Nothing else was a secret. He didn't understand why she needed all of him, to love him the way he needed to be loved. It wasn't just about her happiness, it was also about his.

It took this moment for him to realize it. He gave her more than she was prepared for. He talked about the beatings, the name calling, the starvations, the jumping in place for hours as a form of punishment. He told her everything he had been beaten with, the belts, wooden kitchen spoons, extension cords, telephone cords, curtain rods, fishing poles, wooden paddles. He told her how he was burned with cigarettes, hot combs and choked unconsciously.

As tears poured from his eyes, he tried to explain some of the reasons behind the beatings. Things like if he came home with a D on his report card, or forgetting to take out the trash, or the times when he didn't come fast enough when she called him. Raheem tried to explain to Niama, how hard he tried to be a perfect child. How he tried to stop doing whatever it was that made his mother so angry. He got good grades, perfect attendance awards, and stayed on top of his chores. He even locked himself away in his room, out of sight, and out of mind. It didn't seem to matter. She always found something. She always found an excuse to destroy him. He needed Niama to understand the weight he was carrying back then. Not only was he carrying the extra weight of his home life, but even in high school when peer pressure is at its heights. The kids would clown him about his outdated clothes and he couldn't really make friends because he was afraid his mother would embarrass him. He totally dismissed having a girlfriend. All of this while trying to be this fucking perfect student. Raheem didn't like going to school with bruises and pretending they were from some other source outside of his home. He constantly lied to his classmates, telling them that his bruises were from fist fights with gang members, or his martial arts training sessions. Until one day he couldn't take it anymore. One day he decided it was going to be her or him. He had to be free of her, because she was slowly killing him. He had already tried suicide once, nearly breaking his back when the beam gave way to his weight.

One night he sat outside of her bedroom door with a baseball bat, waiting for her to come out. He was going to set himself free. He was going to set his brother and sister free from their pain. She never came out. Instead in the middle of the night, he opened the back door.

Started running.

And kept running.

And running.

CHAPTER 6

Answers

Nia (short for Niama) just laid there in silence as she listened. Picturing a little boy being tortured, being raped, being beaten, and being destroyed. Story after story of nothing but pure pain and horror. She couldn't take it anymore. It became too much for her empathic soul. Her tears soaked his shirt. The only comfort she could give, was to hold him tighter.

She felt his fear, his agony… she felt his suffering. She could hear the cracking of his voice as he tried to ward off the tears. She could hear the pauses in his speech, in attempts to control his anger. She was getting the answers she believed they needed to be a better couple. Niama never thought it would be answers filled with so much pain. She couldn't hear another word. Being a mother herself, being a woman of God, being a decent human. How can someone treat their own children in such a manner? Those thoughts kept running

51

though her mind. It was almost unbelievable what she was hearing. If it wasn't for what she witnessed, and her two sons, she would have had to give a pause. Nia gently placed her hand to cover his mouth, to let her husband know, she believed him. She didn't need to hear another word. The awkward silence in the room became a blessing. Her brain kept picturing the images he had described. She understood better the scars on his body, she thought it was just from a normal life of hard working and rough housing. They were her husband's personal reminders of pain and abuse. How can a mother be so cruel to her own child? How could a mother take her frustrations out on the body of her own flesh and blood? How?.... Why? ... it didn't make any sense. Niama started to understand her husband better. Things like why he didn't allow many people to get close to him. (If you can't trust your parents who can you really trust). All this time she thought he was just being antisocial.

He was just keeping a safe distance from anyone who could possibly hurt him. She now understood why he preferred cuddling on the couch with her for his birthday. Moments like those were more of a gift than anything she could ever buy for him. Love was the one thing he never received as a child. That's all he needed to feel appreciated, to feel human. Her years of being frustrated because of all the barely used gifts, and believing he didn't like them, stopped after hearing how his mother would beat them, and then take them shopping as an apology. Of course, gifts would become meaningless. The answers she sought after started rushing onto her like waves. Her brain was making connections that explained her husband's nature, like why he never spanked his children. She always thought that he wanted to be the good parent while making her out to be the bad one. This was one of the few things in their marriage that aggravated her. He just didn't want to hit his kids, because he remembered how that made him feel both physically and emotionally. She now believed a part of him was scared that he would go too far and become a monster. He barely raised his voice at them, he had a way of disciplining them with his tone and stare. Naima was actually envious because she had to tell her boys two or three times to do something. Their father would say it once and it was done. The one time she ever heard him go off on them was when their oldest Najm and the youngest Jamal were playing video games. They were about eight and six years old. Najm started calling his baby brother stupid for doing something or not doing something in the game. Jamal retaliated by calling his brother stupid also. Before Nia could say a word, her husband rushed over to them, grabbed them both by their shirts, lifted them in the air, and spoke in a tone they had never heard before.

"If I ever hear either of you call each other by anything other than your names I am going to beat your ass! Am I understood? You are brothers, and you are all you got in this world. Do you understand?!"

Nia remembered being scared for her sons if they didn't answer correctly. The only other time she had seen her husband become that version is when he felt as though somebody was disrespecting her. He got that guard dog look in his eyes and then there was no more mister nice guy.

After hearing some of his horrible story, she felt as though she loved him more. To have gone through as much as he did and still become a gentleman. To be loving and compassionate. To be spiritual and a damn good father. To be patient and playful. It spoke volumes about him, he could have easily become the worst version of himself. He could have used his childhood as an excuse and who besides the prison system would understand? Instead, he is someone she felt blessed every day to have met, married and to raise children with. Which made her feel worse because if she would have listened to him and not tricked him to come back here, things would be different.

She swore it would be good for him, for him to face whatever demon real or not and reconnect to his roots. She couldn't accept that he was happy with just his children and herself. Nia and her mother talked every day, she sees her sister at least three times a month. Talks with her cousins all the time. Hell, she was still in contact with childhood friends. Her Husband, on the other hand, was the exact opposite. He had one friend, Duane and never spoke about any other family. His weekends and vacations were spent with her family. He went to almost every event and supported her side of their family the best he could. He constantly told her that they were all he needed. Now she realized why, they were a part of his new life. One without reminders of pain, abuse and sadness. They were untainted. He could look in their faces and see a present and possible future he didn't think he would ever have. By bringing them here she now realizes that he has been broken.

Her sons had been introduced to a pain they never knew existed and will never forget. Their father would always be reminded that he didn't protect them from the evil he knew existed. Nia couldn't shake the feeling that she had been tricked. Right from the beginning, a simple direct message in her Facebook account. Stating "how beautiful her grand babies looked." Shocking and a pleasant surprise to hear from her unknown mother-in-law. For the last few months, she kept up a secret relationship, with a woman who acted as though she had no clue as to why they didn't have a relationship.

She acted as though the problem was more her son's fault, rather than hers. So many years have passed, and she could not remember what caused him to run away from home. Plus, he had a sister that he hadn't seen since she was a young girl. Nia kept it hidden that they had been face chatting and texting each other almost every single day. She would send Nia recipes and tell little crazy cute stories about her husband. That he never shared with her. Her boys seemed to love the idea that they had two grandmothers. They were excited at the possibility of meeting her. Which was probably why they kept the secret successfully from their father.

Her husband's mother seemed excited, so excited at the idea of forming some sort of relationship with her grandsons before she passed on. She never once gave Nia any clue of what she had done to her husband or what evil she was capable of doing. She believed they had the normal mother son disagreement and both of them were just too stubborn to say sorry. Nia believed, once they laid eyes upon each other and remembered the love, the good old days, and the joyful memories, all would be forgiven, and her deception would not have been in vain.

Instead, Nia was on the phone checking on her sons to see how their wounds were looking. Promising she would pick them up soon and assuring them that they don't have to come back there.

Nia then took the phone to their father and she listened as he reassured them that they weren't in trouble. She let her husband speak to them in private, he understood exactly how they were feeling. She couldn't stand to hear the pain coming from their voices.

She walked into the hall and noticed that Mae, the grandmother had managed to sit herself up and brace herself against a wall. Niama took her a glass of water and sat across from her. She noticed that Mae no longer looked like this sweet, non-threatening older woman. She could actually see the evil behind her eyes.

"Why did you beat my sons?"

CHAPTER 7

Baby Brother (Part One)

Niama sat across from the woman, fighting the urge to lunge at her and beat her like she beat her children. She wondered if she was a stranger, a day care worker or school teacher. Would she already had her hands around her neck getting some sort of retribution? Maybe it was because she was the mother of her husband, the grandmother of her children, or maybe the fear of her Creator was the thing holding her back. Whatever it was, she could feel the grip of patience loosening as she was trying to stay focus. Niama asked again, the question she already knew the answer too. She just wanted to see if truthful words could come from this woman's mouth. Even if they were words of pure malice and hatred, words of some sort of twisted revenge. Niama could make some sense out of that. She could reconcile the woman as crazy, or at least undiagnosed bipolar. Niama was not going to tolerate a lie. She was not going to allow this woman to insult her intelligence anymore and continue to be disrespectful towards her children.

Naima actually knew what happened and exactly what her sons were doing because, it happens almost every day in her house. For at least four months out of the year, for the last two years, when Najm turned eight, his dad put him in Pop Warner football. Najm loved it, since Najm loved it, his baby brother loved it as well. Jamal which they nicknamed 'Shadow' because wherever or whatever his big brother was doing, Jamal was right there. Even when they were toddlers they had to sleep together. The big brother always looked after the little one. Whatever Najm learned, he passed it down to his brother. Which made Jamal a little ahead of everyone else in whatever he did. Nai credited her husband for that, because when Najm was still in diapers he would talk with him about everything. Life, religion, even politics, nothing was taboo. He did the same thing with Jamal, often she would find all three of them knocked out in their bed, her husband would be covered with both of them laying across him one way or another. Still in his work clothes, because they would swarm him the moment he walked through the door. God forbid her husband doing a quick grocery run or something. The boys would break their necks, running around crying because they wanted to go with their father. Their father got a kick out of it, he would sometimes pretend to already have left, just to see their happy faces when he opened the door and say, "let's go!"

One day after a long work week she tried to give her husband a break and keep the boys from disturbing his rest. He told her, "I love it. I want my boys to be able to come to me whenever, talk about whatever, and I never want them to be afraid of me. Respect yes, but never afraid."

As parents, they rarely had to weed through a lie when it came to their boys. So, when Jamal explained to his mother, that they weren't doing anything wrong, he was too adamant and too emotional to be lying.

After their aunt brought them back to the house from sight-seeing, their grandma asked her to go pick up something from the store. Their aunt told them to get dressed again, but their grandma insisted they should stay. It makes no sense to get them all dressed up to do a ten-minute little trip. Their aunt told them to stay in the living room on the couch until she got back. The living room television didn't have cable so there was nothing to watch.

Najm had a thing he loved to do whenever he was bored. He would do walk through drills that his football coach taught the team. On days that the practice field wasn't available they would simply call out the team plays and walk through each player's assignment. This way they both knew what each other was supposed to do. Since Jamal knew the playbook also, he was calling the plays to his brother. As Najm walked through the play, he was telling Jamal where and what each teammate was supposed to do on the play. Their grandma kept screaming into the room from the back to stop running in her house. Jamal said, they told her that they weren't running, that Najm was just doing a walk through.

The next thing they knew she came in, screaming at them, "Do you think I'm stupid?" She knows what running looks like. Jamal said he never left the couch; he was just watching his brother. Najm was trying to explain to his grandmother what he was doing. She kept accusing him of lying. She started yelling louder, about how disrespectful Najm was for talking back to her. Then she said that they needed to be taught a lesson. She left and they didn't understand what she was talking about.

Then she came back with a cord wrapped around her fist and she started hitting Najm. Najm started to run around trying to get away from her but she kept cutting him off. Then she hit him three or four times. Jamal jumped at her and tried to take the extension cord away from her. He wanted her to stop hitting his brother. They wrestled over the extension cord and she threw him off, that's when the items on her table went flying everywhere. Jamal said, that is when she really got mad and started screaming that they were trying to tear up her house. Jamal said, she trapped him in corner, but she really couldn't get to him because the television was blocking her, so she pulled it down out of her way. Then she started hitting him with the cord. Najm came over and covered him with his body. He couldn't keep track of how many times she hit him, all he knew was when their aunt came home. She grabbed her mother and pulled her away. Najm and him ran out of the house, halfway down the block. Their aunt tried to get them to come back inside but they refused. She put us in the car and drove us here.

Niama knew everything, she could still feel the energy of her baby son crying. As he tried to explain as best he could, what happened. She could still hear his words through the tears. It took her a while to settle him down, get him calm enough to check on his scars. He wasn't as bad as her oldest son; the tough one, 'Mr. always got to be tough like his father.' In Naima's mind she could still see the whelps and bruises forming on his back and arms. She watched as his aunt's girlfriend applied ointment on the scars and gave him something to calm down and help them both sleep for a while. Although she had to race after her husband to try and stop him from doing God only knows what. First, she needed to make sure her babies were going to be okay. How did a day that started out so peaceful get crazy in a matter of moments, she thought to herself? How did a trip across the country meant to unite, actually cause more damage? A simple plan, to understand her husband better and bring family unity.

He wasn't himself from the moment they stepped through the front door of the house that he grew up in. He barely came out of their guest room. He wouldn't allow the boys to go anywhere without him. Niama thought he was just being difficult because, he didn't want to be there.

By the second day he couldn't relax, even though this moment was supposed to be a vacation. He seemed more stressed than ever, and he worked damn hard and many long hours. She asked Keisha, her husband's baby sister to take the boys early Sunday morning out sight-seeing or something, so they could have some alone time. Maybe she could figure out what was wrong with him?

When she woke him up and he noticed the boys were gone, he seemed to be relieved that it was just them. His sister told Niama she would have them back by three. They decided to get something to eat. They drove around and he showed her some of his hometown. The more time she spent away from that house, flashes of who she knew her husband to be were coming back. He started to lose his frown, and begin to be his silly, romantic self with her. She wanted to ask him, what was really going on?

Naima reflected on their first night at dinner, it was unnatural to see someone sit across from their mother and not say one word. As though she was invisible, she carried on a conversation with everyone else at the table. It was so strange to Naima, she caught his mother's sly comments and the little digs at him as though she was trying to a get a reaction. Her husband either was immune to it, use to it, or really didn't give a damn. Naima dismissed her as an old woman who didn't know how to talk to her son who she hadn't seen in over twenty years. She didn't want to mess up the trip, when he seemed to be relaxed and happy.

Then just like that, a frantic phone call telling them to meet at some unknown house. The happiness was over. As Niama stared at this woman, thinking about her children and the bruises on their bodies. Her youngest shaking uncontrollably, and her oldest trying to be tough. She became nauseous from all the anger inside of her. She wanted to grab the very extension cord that she hit her sons with and beat her. Give her a taste of it. Rip her skin open and leave marks on her body. Leave her to heal in pain. Niama also wanted to know why, and how someone could do that to children? To her own grandchildren. What is going on inside her mind?

Niama tried asked her again, "why did you beat my children like that, what in the fuck could they had done to deserve that?"

There was no answer in all the universe to justify her actions. Naima needed an answer. The woman, her husband's mother, her children's grandmother said without looking at Niama... "I warned them bad ass kids to stop running in my house!" There it was. The snap of the restraint. Naima, from a sitting position, launched herself at the old woman. Got her hands around her neck and tried to squeeze the life out of her. Screaming at her, "that is no fucking reason! You crazy bitch, that is no fucking reason!"

CHAPTER 8

Baby Brother (Part Two)

Raheem was struggling with his wife, who kept screaming at him, "let me the fuck go!" A part of him wanted to let her take out their frustration on the very person who caused it. At his core he couldn't allow her to also be dragged down. He couldn't allow her to be equally as worst as his mother. He needed her to understand something, she needed to understand what he has been carrying around for far too long.

He gently but forcibly led her down the short flight of stairs, toward the basement bedrooms. As Naima unsuccessfully struggled against her husband's grip, she hated that he was so damn strong. She kept screaming at him, this time saying, that she didn't need to see where his mother use to abuse her children. She had all the proof she needed and wanted to finish teaching her a lesson. He didn't say a word as he led her through the dimly lit hallway.

Naima was familiar with this part of the house because Keisha, her sister-in-law, showed her the rooms when they first arrived. Keisha assumed her older brother would want privacy for his family. This level of the house had two bedrooms, a small kitchen, a bathroom, and a decent size living room. Keisha and Naima were really surprised when he decided his family was going to share one tiny room upstairs together. Now Naima realized why having the boys in the same room was more-so for their protection.

Naima was pleading with him. She didn't need to see where his mother damn near put his head through a wall or tied him to a door and beat him unconscious. She actually had enough of these stories. He ignored her and lead her into the second bedroom, his baby brother's old room. It basically had nothing inside but a bed and a small dresser. Naima knew her husband's brother died at a young age.

He never told her how, or what effect his death had on him. Just like everything else that dealt with his past he stayed silent especially anytime his baby brother would come up. This immense sadness would overcome her husband's energy, and he would shut down. Most times he would just change the subject or walk away. Raheem gently sat her down on the bed and sat next to her. She knew whatever this was that it was serious to him. He had certain idiosyncrasies, that usually gave away his moods. When he's being silly his eyes lit up, or when he was extremely angry, he would breathe heavier like a bull. Right now, he is in deep contemplation, she noticed his hands in both pockets, extremely quiet with his head down and eyes closed. They sat there for about five minutes, she looked at him watching tears fall from his eyes. Naima was confused but tried to be patient and give her husband the time he needed. He begun to speak, in slow measured tones.

"On that wall there was a poster of Bruce Lee, you know, The Enter the Dragon, the one with claw scratches on his body. I actually got that for him around his tenth birthday. He was crazy about karate. On that wall was a poster of the Teenage Mutant Ninja Turtles. The dumbest movie ever, but he loved that damn thing. On that dresser was a trophy, his baseball team finished first, he was the MVP. He was so annoying for months, because that was the one trophy I never won." "MVP, MVP," he would chant whenever he wanted to get on my nerves." Niama noticed her husband would smile every time he recalled a memory.

"He used to get on my nerves so bad. He had asthma and my mother got her hands on this huge humidifier about the length of this bed, it took like five big buckets of water to fill it up. He always waited until the middle of the night to walk in my room, waking me with his heavy breathing. Talking about he needed water to be put in his tank. Every time I would ask him why he didn't check before bed. I didn't think about it… every time I wanted to jump up and kick his little ass. He would always say,"

"Thank you, bro, I love you."

"I would always respond, "yeah… yeah… yeah."

The same response Niama has heard over the years when she has said those same words to him.

"That night I ran away from home I didn't take anything with me. I didn't think to pack clothes or shoes. I just opened the door and left. I honestly think I ran about twenty blocks before I stopped. I was so afraid, and in the back of my mind I kept thinking that she was right behind me. So, I did all these crazy zig zag patterns. Two blocks east, then a block west , then maybe five blocks south. It was crazy cause I was running through unknown gang territories and known drugs areas. I was more afraid of her catching me and bringing me back to this house then being shot down by some street punk. That night I actually slept in one of those over size dumpsters, the odor has never left my nose. I was so nauseous that night because of that fucking dumpster.

Since my mother didn't know anything about our lives, I was able to hang out at a friend's house from time to time. I don't think she knew I had any friends. They were never allowed to come over and we were never allowed out. I think if she could have home schooled us, she would have. My only friend Duane, let me sleep on his floor. On days that he would be back too late to let me in, he would leave his bedroom window unlocked and I would technically break into his bedroom to sleep. He tried to give me some of his old clothes, but he was two sizes bigger than me. Somethings I could pull off, somethings I couldn't, but the laughter from my classmates, I had to deal with. All I needed to do is get through my junior year. One more year of school, then I could get my GED and get a job. Hell, even join the Army. I just needed to get through one more school year.

So, every Friday I would meet my brother after his school let out. I don't think my mom remembered that on Fridays the school ended thirty minutes earlier than usual. On those days I would get to spend those few minutes with my bro. He would sneak me a pair of jeans or a sweatshirt. He couldn't bring them to me all at once. He said our mother locked most of my clothes up. Stating that it was her money that brought those clothes, which makes them hers. Somehow, he was able to sneak out somethings for me. Knowing if she caught him it would be hell to pay.

Every Friday my brother would beg to go with me. He told me that she had gotten worse. The beating had gotten worse and she kept blaming it on me. Saying if I would come home, she would stop.

I couldn't come home. I couldn't bring myself to walk back into that life. Even though I was sleeping on someone else's floor. Spending my weekends hiding in libraries and parks, riding the bus from one end to another, over and over again. I was eating soup line meals and begging for spare change. It was better than living in fear, every single moment. I couldn't bring him with me, where could I go with him that was safe? How could I explain why he wasn't in school? Where would he sleep?

I tried to explain my plan to him, I tried to explain that I haven't forgotten about him. I just needed time, a little time to get my head together. I needed to figure something out, because I... I... didn't want to get hit again. I asked him to be strong for a little while longer. I had put up with it for sixteen years... just give me one more year, please.

One Friday he didn't show up. I figured he was mad at me and just went straight home. I honestly respected that, I understood. Going through the abuse... you feel so alone. I decided to risk it and go to see him at home. I knocked, knocked and knocked. But nothing. I figured, maybe he is with my mom and my sister shopping or something.

Fuck, I said to myself. I broke into my house through the kitchen window. The moment my feet touched the floor, I got this eerie feeling. I didn't quite know what it was, maybe the fear of being caught? Or simply being back inside this hell pit?

I knew I didn't have much time. I rushed down the stairs, heading to my room, I am already mentally picturing everything I wanted to grab. As I... As I... was... passing this room... his room... out of the corner of my eye...I could see my baby brother.

Naima never saw her husband cry like he did, she was actually frozen and didn't know whether to hold him or allow him to get it out.

"I could... see him... just... hanging there in the middle of the room... he was just there... ooh... ooh... I screamed no bro!... No bro...nooo!... Please, no bro! I rushed to him and I tried to get him down. I called out to God to help me. Help me get my brother down... please God! It was like God said you left him... why do you care now?! But I kept trying... and I couldn't get him down.

Then I heard her coming through the door and I got scared. So many fucked up thoughts started running through my head. What if she blames this one on me? I honestly couldn't put it past her. I grabbed some clothes out of my room, and I snuck back out. My coward ass... left my baby brother hanging from this fucking ceiling. I should have come back for that one year. Put up with the abuse, all of it, for one more year. Then he would still be alive. I would have been there to take some of the pain. Maybe that is why I survived for so long... he was always there with me.

Do you know what she told people? She told people that my brother died in his sleep. Had some sort of mysterious illness. Fucking bitch... she couldn't let people find out that her youngest boy killed himself, to get away from her. One already left home, she could explain that as drugs, or being rebellious. She couldn't explain the second one dying like that... you know... she couldn't explain that to her church... she was miss goodie two shoes. Bible thumping, catching the Holy

Ghost every Sunday. Promising to be better, swearing in the name of her God, to be a better human. She would walk right into the house after church in the same damn Sunday's best outfits and beat her children like they were curses from God."

CHAPTER 9

The Beginning of the Ending

Niama just sat there looking at her husband. He had his arms and legs crossed, his head hanging down. She watched as his tears hit the floor. Thinking to herself, how has he been carrying around this burden for years. She was trying to think of some magical words to say to him to ease his grief and to take away his pain, but she couldn't think of anything. The words, it's not your fault or you have to let that go didn't seem to fit. No hug, kiss or anything that she could possibly do could make her husband forgive himself, only he had the power to do that. Only he could release himself from the belief his brother would still be alive if he would have come back home. Niama realized that coming back to this house refreshed a horrible memory. She watched her six-foot-tall, construction working, strong as an ox husband cry like she has never seen him before. He was hurting. Hurting in a place she could not help. Hurting in a way that she had no knowledge or understanding of. She could not think of a Biblical verse or Quranic word that would make sense of it all. She couldn't think of anything that would free her husband of guilt. What made her feel worse is that she couldn't really empathize with him, because she knew of no one close to her who had committed suicide. Niama couldn't even imagine one of her sisters ending their lives that way. Let alone living with the image of one of them hanging from a ceiling. Since she couldn't get emotionally there with him, a part of her felt useless.

For the first time in her marriage, Niama felt as though she was letting her husband down. The corner stone in her mind, what made them successful was that they always had each other's back. When one of them went down for whatever reason, the other naturally stepped up. Now, he was somewhere she couldn't reach. Niama decided the only option that would be good for her family was to leave. She said to him "babe lets go… we can go upstairs… pack our bags… go get our boys and take the next plane home." She waited patiently for his response. After a while when he didn't respond…

she said it again, "let's just go babe." Niama stood up, reached for her husband's hand, and gently tried to pull him towards the door.

Raheem responded,

"You know when we came here, I had all these thoughts and emotions running through me. I was so... scared of that woman. So, scared of what she might do to us. I realized just now... I was afraid of the wrong thing."

Raheem stood up and wiped his tears from his face. He gave out a small yell, as if he was shaking off a sharp pain after bumping into something. He then leaned down and kissed his wife with all the love he had in his heart. Then he said,

"Babe do you trust me?"

He looked his wife straight in the eyes. Naima knew that look, the look of determination. Which in some cases could be a good thing, but on this day, in this moment she wasn't sure.

"What do you mean, do I trust you?" Niama responded with nervousness in her voice.

"Like I asked you. Do you trust me?"

Niama knew she didn't need to answer that question. Something about her husband was different though. He seemed too eerily calm, like right before a tornado. The way he was looking into her eyes made her feel uncomfortable. She answered the only way she could.

"Of course, I trust you… and you know that… but I am scared."

She pulled her husband close to her and tried to hug him with all the love in her soul. Letting him know that she needed him, and whatever he was thinking wasn't worth jeopardizing their family and the life they had built together.

Raheem felt every word, he noticed the fear in her eyes. He didn't want to lose his family, the only true loves he ever had in his life. Though he wanted to honestly calm her fears he truly couldn't tell her everything was going to be alright. One thing about their relationship is that he had never technically told her a lie. He would just not say anything, he thought it was the best of his options. Now he realized that not telling her everything was actually worst. Not telling her, wasn't for his benefit, it was for him not to have to deal with all the pain buried inside of him. He was actually protecting himself and guarding whatever positive image she had of him. Not understanding she needed to love all of him, and not just the smooth areas. It was a great fear of his to allow her into that part of him, because it was the one thing that scared him the most.

He knew he had to sit face to face with his living demon. Destroy the power she had over him. So, he can truly live and allow his wife and children to love him completely and gain full access to his heart and life. Sitting in that room he realized that he loved his children so much that he had done everything possible to ensure their happiness. He had also been keeping a part of himself a secret because he was worried about making that one bad decision that would scar them for the rest of their lives. Though he loved his wife and knew how lucky he was to have met her, there was a part of him that wouldn't allow her in. That part of him that had been beaten down to the point it couldn't take another hit. The part of him that has been broken for so long that it had become a natural part of his life. It was time to fix it.

He looked at her and told her… "I need you to pack the bags and wait outside for our children." He didn't wait for a response, he simply walked out of the room and headed up the stairs. She slowly followed behind him; she watched as he went to the kitchen and searched though the drawers for something. She couldn't see what he put in his pocket. Niama raced into the guest room and started throwing things in the suitcases, nervous about what her husband was thinking about doing.

The wife and mother in her wanted to stand right next to him to ensure that he didn't do anything stupid. The wife and mother in her also knew she needed to trust him and believe that his love for his family was greater than the pain he carried. He just stood back and watched as Niama carried the bags out of the front door. He gave her a kiss on the forehead and locked the door behind her.

He slowly walked over to the short hallway where his mother was still sitting, half leaning against the wall.

He sat right across from her and for the first time in a long while he looked her right in the eyes.

CHAPTER 10

God

He sat there for a moment listening to his mother praying. Reciting various verses from her Holy book. As though she was giving herself the last rites. He couldn't help but to chuckle.

"The more things change the more they stay the same," he said to her. She momentarily stopped but continued and even raised her tone.

"Surprisingly the very God you are praying to, I stop believing in because of you," he said making sure to maintain eye contact with her avoiding glances.

"It's strange to me how a person can pray for mercy and forgiveness, can be the same person who is void of those very things. I still can't reconcile that, it is like the perfect conundrum. There you sit asking God for protection. You know you fucked up, and you might need a miracle to get you out of this one." His mother stopped for a moment then she begin to say something but changed her mind.

"Do you remember when I was about twelve, you sent us to church the Sunday before Christmas. You made Dee and I go and pray for a better life. While you "entertained" your boyfriend. I have never forgotten that day, because the preacher gave a sermon about hurting the children of God. It will be like putting a milestone noose around your neck and being thrown in the ocean. The preacher said, so if anyone is hurting God's children then they will be punished. I can still remember thinking God must not know about Dee and me. Right then the preacher said if you're being hurt come on Christmas Eve and God will be here and you can tell him.

"I thought that was our chance. I waited all week for Wednesday night. I got dressed for church. You asked me where I was going. I told you I was going to church. I walked out the house, I was scared that you were going to stop me. Like you knew I was going to go and tell God on you. I can feel you watching me walk, but I refused to turn around.

"I got to church, and I sat in the front row. I listened to every poem about Jesus, every Christmas song, and I mean songs I had no idea existed. I listened to so many testimonies about the power of God and how he changed his children's lives. I was encouraged, and impatient, I kept looking for him wondering when he was going to show up. Then the preacher said, 'it's time.' He told us to bow our heads and close our eyes and whatever the problem is, picture it in our mind. Ask God to remove it. I pictured every slap, every punch, every time you purposely sent us to bed hungry. How you beat us when we got caught looking for food. I pictured the time you urinated on me. Who fucking does that to a child? While I was picturing these things, I was praying to God to please remove us from you because I feared we would die. I prayed for us to be put with strangers because you hated us. I prayed so hard that tears and sweat flowed down my face. I overheard one usher say, 'whatever that young man is praying for he should get.' I opened my eyes to see if God was listening. I couldn't see him, the preacher said he left but he heard my prayers.

I left that church filled with this unbelievable sense of relief. Like this giant burden had been lifted. When I walked in this house, I believed it was going to be my last time. That God was going to knock on our door and take us away. That we were going to go someplace safe where you could never find us. I remember walking past you thinking you are in trouble, God knows, God knows all about you. I can remember singing that church hymn *"Jesus on the main line telling him what you want."* I sang that song all the way from church, right past you, down the stairs and as I was changing clothes."

"Jesus on the main line tell him what you want," then you busted into my room with an extension cord in hand and you screamed at me…

'What did you go to church for!?'

"I told you the truth, to see God, to see Jesus. And you swore I was lying. Then you started to beat me with that cord, telling me to tell you the truth. I told you to see Jesus, over and over again. I kept looking at the door waiting for him to come through and stop you because I believed I was one of his children and you was hurting me. He didn't show up and you kept beating me. Then it clicked, Jesus had to be your God, to allow you to get away with all you was doing. I, we, were nothing to him." His mother stopped chanting. Because of you I have a problem with God and the forgiveness aspect of life. I can't forgive you. Maybe if he would have showed up and saved us then I would be more open to the concept. You are evil. For me to say I forgive you is like giving you a pass on all the pain you have caused. I would be saying to you that it is okay, when it's not. You broke me, you broke me in ways I will never heal from. I will never forget... and I can never forgive. I have so many scars on my body from you that at times I refuse to look at myself. I don't understand why, because you and my father didn't work out? You decided to have sex and get pregnant, so we too had to suffer? I don't understand. Please explain to me what I did to you to deserve all of what you did? Please tell me why? So, I can understand, why your God deemed it fitting for you to hurt us in the ways you did. Then maybe I can forgive you and God."

His mother said nothing. She just sat there with tears running down her face. They sat in silence for minutes. She seemed to be searching for words, he was waiting for words. All she could do was start chanting her mantra again.

"I thought so. The crazy thing is, when I saw the scars you put on my babies, on my children, I knew I had to kill you. I was going to be damned if they were going to suffer like my brother and me. I am not going to allow them to fall for that line you used to say, "I am sorry, I just love you so much or it won't happen again." While I was driving here, I was praying to your God and telling him, if you don't want me to kill her you better stop me. You better make it difficult to get to her. Surprisingly, I made every single light. Cars seemed to moved out of my way. There was even a parking spot in front of the house. I just swooped the car in, without any trouble. When I saw you peek out of the curtains, I said one more prayer for you. I told your God this is your last chance, you better lock that door. I guess your God has grown tired of you, because that door couldn't hold me back. When you tried to run from me it reminded me of those many times, I tried to run from you. My heart filled with this same rage and I could see myself pulling the back of your hair so hard and smashing your face into a wall. The moment before I could grab you, you would slip and fall, and there I stood over you. As much as I wanted to hit you and stomp you through this floor, I couldn't, I just couldn't hit you. I couldn't hit my mother. What the fuck is wrong with me? Though everybody in the world would have understood. I couldn't hit you, instead I wanted to help you. What did I get in return for that kindness? You cut my hand with a fucking piece of glass.

CHAPTER 11

Fire

"Here we are, two broken humans. How do we fix this?" Raheem asked, as he stared at his mother. "For so long I have thought about this moment, crazy enough I knew it would end in death. Maybe that is why I have been avoiding it for so long… today, it has to end."

Raheem stood up and reached his hand out for his mother. She hesitated for a moment looking into his face for any signs of aggression. He gently helped her up and gave her a hug.

"That's for giving me life, not because I love you. Because if not for my life, I wouldn't have met my beautiful wife and had my sons. I truly thank you for that." He led his mother by the hand and they slowly walked toward the back bedroom, her room. "I used to hate coming in here, I cannot think of one good memory being in this room. Every time you would call me in here, I would get nauseous, I hated this room." Raheem slowly pulled out of his pocket the item he pulled from the kitchen drawer.

He let his mother's hand go and walked her towards her bedroom curtains. "You know, it would be at the weirdest times when the memories of what you did to me would flood my mind. A breeze, a smell, even some songs that just popped on the radio. Like a plug-in, damn I'd weaken, and I would just get washed with all the filth and pain. In this room is where it all started, you know I can still remember how you smelled. Sick, right? No son should know how his mother's pussy smells." His mother noticed the electric lighter in his hand, and he began to set her bedroom curtains on fire. She started to yell at him but the look in his eyes told her it would be useless.

"I hate this room!"

Raheem stood for a moment and watched the flames start to spread across the walls. He gently grabbed her hand and lead her into the next room. "In this room, you remember you actually sat on my head and suffocated me until I passed out. I think that was the day I asked you about my father?" Just like the previous room, he went towards the curtains and lit them on fire.

"I hated this room too," he chuckled.

He walked toward the kitchen, opened the oven door and blew out the pilot lights. Raheem turned on the gas.

"I am taking away the one thing from you, your biggest deception. This house, because people saw the nice the furniture, the big televisions and how clean you kept it. They thought this house was one of peace and love. In actuality, it was a part of hell on earth. You have to pay for all you have done, you too must suffer. Then maybe you can start to understand how you broke your own children."

He led her from the kitchen to the living room. He made his way through the broken glass and shattered television, looking for something. He bent down and pulled from the wreckage a photo album. Raheem opened it and started smiling while tears ran down his face.

"I am taking this, these pictures of my brother that you pushed to end his life. You can stay in this house as it burns down around you, or you can grab you a coat and figure out what your next step is going to be."

He went around the living room setting the curtains on fire. "Any way you choose, I don't give a damn. Don't come near my family again or I will kill you. Did I say it like you did? Anyway, consider yourself lucky."

Raheem walked out of the front door. He met his sister as she was trying to go inside to grab her mother. Gave her a big hug and whispered into her ear, "I am sorry, if you need anything, call me. You are welcome to come live with us, we have plenty of space and there are plenty of jobs in Seattle. Don't go into that house it's not safe." She looked at him and nodded her head yes to let him know she understood. They both looked at the house, the flames, and smoke overtaking the place. There in the big window of the living room stood their mother. Keisha was screaming for her to get out of the house. Naima came from the rental car and gave her husband a hug and lead him back to the car. He got in and looked back at his sons who were knocked out sleep.

He half listened to his wife as she explained that they could fly out tonight or early tomorrow. As he put the car into gear and begin to drive away. He noticed his mother standing in the window watching as he began to drive away, within moments the house exploded.

CHAPTER 12

Closure

Rayheem stood at the headstone of his baby brother. It was surreal to see his brother's name etched in stone and the years between his birth and death so close together. It brought tears to Raheem's eyes.

"Hey Baby Bro. It's been a long time. I am sorry I haven't visited you. I guess I was ashamed to face you. I knew I should have been there for you. I was being selfish and trying to protect my own sanity. I'm sorry, I shouldn't have left you alone to deal with all of that, I hope you can forgive me. Have you seen your nephews? They remind me of us so much. Always trying to outdo one another, it's so funny. I swear Jamal looks just like you, he makes those silly faces that you did. I feel that you are still here with me more than just in memory. I want to tell you something, I never really said to you when you were around. I really loved you, even on the days you got on my last nerves. I wished to God we could have grown up in a different home, I swear we would have been whatever we wanted. We got cheated at becoming the tag team champions of the world. Baby Bro I have to go now, I have a plane to catch. Don't think I don't think about you. I do every day of my life. See you sooner than later."

Yeah, Yeah, Yeah

The End

We Never Knew

We never knew when you would snap out and beat us,

or damn near kill us.

We walked around on pins and needles.

Stuttered when you spoke to us.

Flinched when you moved too fast.

We never learned how to relax around you.

When you wanted to laugh and play.

We would run and hide

Bust out crying when you call our names.

We never asked you for a good night kiss,

too afraid of the response we may get.

Studied hard for good grades, because we knew

it was for our own sakes.

Never told you about the things that made us happy,

or that we secretly searched for our daddies.

It is sad when we compare our scars.

We still can remember which ones are from you

and which ones are not.

Peace

The End

I received a phone call... today.

The voice said, you passed away.

Awkward silence.

Neither knew what to say.

I immediately felt at peace.

No.

More accurately.

Safer.

No longer would I have to worry about the possibility of an accidental sighting.

Of a blood stranger.

Whose bond should have been greater than the wires that hold up bridges.

Pretending that we meant something to each other.

Acting as though we had joy to had found one another.

In truth one pushed, the other raced.

Our history covered in violence and horrendous secrecy.

That still feels me with unease.

Often having me talking to a professor.

To exorcise my memories and keep the created demons at bay.

How carefully I dream.

I tried to squeeze out a tear.

Have some empathy.

My body wouldn't allow.

It still remembers.

My heart wouldn't allow.

You planted no seeds of love.

My soul...

controversially wouldn't allow.

Now it's truly free of... fear.

Rest in what you reap.

You may have stored more good deeds

that outweigh the damage you done to me.

I will not pray for your peace.

On earth, you didn't allow me to grow in peace.

The End

Made in the USA
Las Vegas, NV
11 February 2022